Broad Haven 1977

By Justin Tully

Copyright Justin Tully 2023

Imagination 1976

All Rights Reserved

Chapter Index

Chapter One: Sighting

Chapter Two: The Men in Black Arrive

Chapter Three: The Morning After

Chapter Four: Night Arrives

Chapter Five: Confrontation

Chapter One

Sighting

Daniel Price was seated in his office while flicking through some paperwork, he'd been putting off doing when someone entered his room without knocking leaving him wondering what on earth was going on.

"What's going on Kelly, because I'm a little bit busy at the moment." He pointed out to her before picking up his paperwork to highlight the fact, but she had urgent information that just wouldn't wait.

"I've just received a telephone call from a Bryony Edwards. She called from a small town called Broad Haven where apparently a group of youngsters saw a UFO type object in the sky."

Kelly advised him and with that he immediately released the paperwork, which fell quickly back onto his desk in a mess.

"I take it she's still on the line?" Daniel asked her in hopeful fashion, but she shook her head to show that she hadn't wished to be on hold.

"Unfortunately, she was going to go out to the local school to talk to some of the teachers there, but I've got her telephone number for when she returns again." Kelly said to him and with that she placed the piece of paper down onto his desk, but he couldn't see how this would be entirely useful since she didn't sound like she'd even be there at this moment.

"Kelly? I want you to grab your coat since we are off to Broad Haven, was it? Where is that again?" Daniel suggested to her and with that Kelly laughed since this was just like Daniel to jump into something without knowing any of the details firsthand.

"Don't worry I'll guide you there, but once we get there, you'll have to do most of the work. Do you want to take my new car?" Kelly wondered what he made of things, and with that they made their way into the car park before getting into Kelly's new car.

"Yes, that sounds like a terrific plan. Did you hear anything from the school itself?" Daniel looked to find out as they got into her car, and she started up the engine on her nineteen seventy-six green coloured mini - cooper.

"So, what else can you tell me about this woman who called, because we're going to have to track her down when we reach Broad Haven." Daniel pointed out to her and with that she passed over a note, which he took from her moments before she started the car.

"Bryony Edwards aged nineteen and currently staying in a boarding house in the middle of Broad Haven. The only thing I'm concerned about is how trusted she is, because the last thing we need to do is going into tearing into town only to find out this whole thing has been a hoax." Daniel explained his position to his friend and secretary who shared the same feelings on the subject, as he did.

"That would reflect badly on the both of us Daniel. I for one happen to believe it, because she certainly sounded shaken up and in my book that means only one thing...she's seen something that can't be forgotten about." Kelly said to him, as they continued - on their way towards Broad Haven with some serious questions for Bryony Edwards and plenty of other people in town for that matter.

"Have you got anything interesting for us to listen to, as we go along since I'm sure we'll run out of conversation sooner or later?" Daniel suggested to Kelly who smiled before reaching down and turning the radio on where they picked up on Wales FM.

"Now is there a more famous Welshman in the world than Tom Jones?" Daniel asked the driver who smiled back in his direction since he was one of her favourites too.

In Broad Haven, Bryony Edwards had just knocked on the door of Turner Hope a member of the National Geological Society, and after several moments he opened the door to his visitor to see what she wanted from him.

"Yes, can I help you with something?" Turner suggested to her, and it was clearly - evident that she had something on her mind judging from the serious expression on her face.

"I've been in contact with a school in the area, and they are telling me that a number of their students had noticed something they didn't believe came from this world in the sky." Bryony informed him, and with that brief description he instantly let her into his office.

"Could I get you a mug of tea or coffee, perhaps?" Turner looked to find out if a pinch of caffeine might help her to relax since she certainly seemed very tense at this time.

"Yes, a coffee would be good. I take mine with two sugars." Bryony advised him, and with that he headed into his kitchen to make their drinks for them, but before he came back, he picked up a telephone that was situated there in - order to call his colleague Roger Hammersley.

"Turner? This was supposed to be my day off. I'm warning you now that this better be good and a worthy use of my time." Roger said to him, but this was important information and Turner felt that it just couldn't wait until he returned to the office again.

"Believe it or not Roger? I've got a Bryony Edwards with me, and she's reporting that numerous school children have sighted something above the school in the sky. Roger...they believe that it's a UFO. What do you make of that idea?" Turner suggested to him, but Roger didn't automatically answer showing that he wasn't leaping for joy at this moment.

"School children at a school? What kind of eyewitnesses would they be when you come to think about it Turner? I mean think about it, they say they've seen something they didn't think was meant to be there, but if we went to Jodie Rollings my newspaper friend with this story, she probably wouldn't take it seriously once we disclose the age of the people involved." Roger reminded him, and with that Turner seemed somewhat deflated on the other end of the line.

"Just don't rule anything out Roger. We can both go to the school concerned tomorrow morning, how does that sound to you?" Turner hoped that he would agree with this idea, and Roger agreed that this did sound like something in theory that needed to be looked - into. Turner brought the mugs of coffee back into the main area of his office where he found Bryony Edwards staring out of the window at the view outside.

"Did you see anything out there?" Turner wondered if she'd made a sighting of her own before he passed her the mug of coffee to drink.

"No. I didn't see anything out there, but it just makes you think, doesn't it? I mean the ideas of a UFO visiting this area of Wales from somewhere unknown sends a cold shiver down the spine don't you agree with me?" Bryony suggested to him before he sat down at his typewriter in - order to take down the details of this particular - incident at least from Bryony even though she wasn't there in the first person to witness the UFO herself.

"Don't you think that you should wait until you interview the school children, because they were the ones that actually saw this thing in the sky?" Bryony took the opportunity to remind him, that she could only regurgitate the information that she'd heard from someone else.

"Point taken Bryony. Also, just to let you know that I've been in touch with my colleague Roger Hammersley and together we'll be heading down to the school tomorrow morning in - order to check the incident out for ourselves. Although having said that I don't think there's going to be anything to be too concerned about. I'm certain that there will be an earthly answer behind this mystery." Turner informed her before they wrote some notes down about this incident, because Bryony found it soothing - and it eased her racing mind.

Jodie Rollings was about to pack up for the day when her black coloured desk telephone started ringing, and even though she didn't want to answer it she decided to pick up anyway.

"Hello? This is Jodie Rollings of the Broad Haven Shore Times?" She greeted her caller in cordial fashion, but she soon found that it was a familiar voice on the other end of the line.

"Jodie! Thank goodness I've caught you, because I know that you usually shoot off for the day around now? Anyway, my colleague Turner Hope has come across a rather fantastic sounding story. We're talking about UFO's seen above a local school in the area." Roger Hammersley announced catching her somewhat on the hop since this sounded rather out there to say the least.

"What are you talking about? I mean UFO'S at a school, and I'm presuming this incident was seen by some school children?" Jodie sought to find out if this was the right conclusion to leap to here, and with that he couldn't say she was in the wrong lane.

"Look I know how it sounds, and I wasn't going to tell you until we found out more information about this incident, but I felt that you'd like to be in this from the ground upwards?" Roger suggested to her and with that she laughed nervously on the other end of the phone.

"In that case you are correct. I'll come with you and your colleague to the Broad Haven school tomorrow morning, because this is some story that sounds like it's got some real legs to it." Jodie confirmed for him before she got off the phone, but instead of leaving the office as planned she instead placed another phone call to someone, she'd recently met at a convention another UFO investigator named Frederick Tate.

"Hello, this is Frederick Tate speaking?" Frederick answered the phone call within three rings always eager to speak to new people.

"Frederick Tate! It's good to speak to you again, this is Jodie Rollings from the Broad Haven Shores Times. We met each other once at a mystery convention while we were both in London." Jodie explained to him, and he smiled on the other end of the line since she sounded like she might have a case for him.

"It's nice to hear from you, but I'm judging from your tone that you aren't calling me to see how I've been doing or what I've been up to recently?" Frederick suggested to her, and she couldn't deny that this was the case since there was an urgent investigation about to get underway in Broad Haven, West Wales.

"I've been informed almost quite literally in fact that a group of schoolchildren have witnessed something amazing in the sky above their school in Broad Haven. I've agreed to go along with my friend Roger Hammersley of the National Geological Survey to the Broad Haven school tomorrow morning where we hope to rule out what it might or might not have been." Jodie explained to Frederick who felt that if they were looking at earthly reasons behind this sighting then they might not need him.

"Has anyone apart from schoolchildren seen this thing, because I don't want to get picky since they don't always make the most credible of witnesses." Frederick pointed out to her, but in the moment, he suddenly realised that this could turn out to be something worth investigating, so despite his reservations he took down the directions to the coastal West Wales town.

Daniel Price and Kelly Evans arrived in the town of Broad Haven before parking in the car park of the Haven Fort Hotel. They proceeded to get out of the car before making their way into the Hotel in - order to book a couple of rooms for the coming days.

"Hello, how can I help you out today?" Tiffany Gibson the lady behind the front desk sought to find out what their requirements were.

"We'd like to book a couple of rooms at the hotel, that's if there are some available of course. We are fully aware that this place could soon be picking up in business over the coming few days." Daniel pointed out to Tiffany who looked perplexed by his comments.

"Why would that be the case? Sorry, but I'm not currently following you. Has something happened that I should be concerned about?" Tiffany suggested to Kelly and Daniel who realised that perhaps not everyone in town had been alerted by the UFO flying over a local school.

"I don't suppose you've heard about any rumours, as it pertains to a UFO seen over a local school just yesterday?" Kelly looked to find out from Tiffany who shrugged her shoulders since she most certainly hadn't heard about anything like that. It made her come over all cold, and that was saying something since she was standing in front of a heater on this cool February day even inside the hotel.

"Did you say that this UFO was seen over a school? If that's the case, then who in the world told you about it?" Tiffany suggested to them, and with that Daniel nominated himself to explain what they knew about the incident.

"Yes. That's the way we heard it. From a lady in this town too." Daniel said to Tiffany who looked very much intrigued, and she looked forward to hearing about who'd called them since she might know who the person was.

"Are you going to tell me who it was or is this a secret?" Tiffany sought to find out, and with that Daniel looked at his assistant to provide the details for her.

"Her name is Bryony Edwards, but we aren't too sure where she lives, but she was the one that raised the alarm for us to venture to Broad Haven." Kelly Evans explained to Tiffany who raised some eyebrows at this disclosure since she knew Bryony Edwards quite well.

"Bryony is a bit of fantasist to be honest with you. Don't get me wrong, but I'd like her to have become involved with something real here. She lives in the hotel here, and you'll probably come across her sooner or later." Tiffany said to them, and in doing so instantly deflated the pair who were there to see what this UFO incident amounted up to.

"Well, in that case we'll just have to hope that she's right on this occasion. We've come a long way to see what the incident involves." Daniel confirmed for Tiffany who smiled sweetly back into their direction before she handed over their room keys to them.

"Do you believe in UFO's yourself Tiffany?" Kelly wondered what kind of person they were dealing with here since she might just be the kind of person who dismisses all such incidents.

"I'm the kind of person who believes things when they see them. Dinner is at five o'clock sharp. Do you need a tour guide to take you around the town or are you happy to just explore yourselves?" Tiffany wondered since she had just the perfect person to show them around if they took her up on her offer.

"Yes, that would be good. Are you going to be showing us around?" Kelly sought to find out, but Tiffany then shook her head to show that wouldn't be the case and with that they looked, as another woman made her way into view.

"Daniel and Kelly this is Davina Walters. She will be more than happy to show you around Broad Haven." Tiffany informed them before they each shook Davina by the hands and then proceeded to place their bags into their hotel rooms.

Davina brought Kelly and Daniel towards the Broad Haven school, the place where the sighting of the UFO was made by the school children. It seemed eerily quiet at this time of the day, and there wasn't anything in the sky at this point other than the odd cloud.

"This place seems so peaceful, and not somewhere where you'd think such a strange event would've taken place?" Kelly suggested to Davina who shrugged her shoulders before she addressed her question.

"From what I could gather it was just like this before the UFO was seen too, so seeing is definitely believing and there are plenty of children who saw it." Davina informed them both before she opened the front door, and then showed them inside. They made their way towards the reception desk where Mrs Helen Pitman was looking over some paperwork. She soon looked up however, and then also adjusted her blue rimmed spectacles, so that she could get a better look at the three people in front of her.

"Yes? What can I do for you today, because my telephone has been ringing off the hook as you can see on the orders of the headteacher we've had to take it off the hook. It's the reason why it's not currently working. If you've come here to ask in person - then that's my answer." Mrs Pitman explained to them, but they weren't particularly interested in the telephone and whether it was working or not.

"My name's is Daniel Price, and this is my assistant Kelly Evans. We've come here today to investigate an incident, which apparently recently took place? Something that concerned a UFO?" Daniel suggested to her, but rather than answer the question instead Mrs Pitman hailed over another one of her colleagues.

"This is Max Davies, and he's got all the answers you're after. So, why don't you follow him into an adjacent office where I'm sure he'll more than satisfy your questions." Mrs Pitman said to them, and with that they followed the aforementioned - Max Davies into the office where he gestured for them all to take some chairs.

"I'd start this out with asking what you want to talk about, but I think that I've already got a very good idea of what you have in mind. Do you want me to share my account with you or are you instead looking to field me some questions?" Max wondered what they had on their minds here and with that Daniel placed his hand in the air like one of the schoolchildren, which wasn't lost on Kelly because she found this amusing.

"How many of the schoolchildren witnessed the UFO, because that's something I'm going to have to place in my report on this incident?" Daniel sought to find out, and with that Max leant back in his chair, as he placed his hands on his own chin.

"There were actually - quite a few of the schoolchildren who witnessed this event. I've been told that there were fourteen of them, but obviously I can't divulge their names to you so that you can't individually interview them. As, people who are in the media such as yourselves you can understand why no students are allowed to talk to you?" Max suggested to them, and with that Davina nodded her head while Kelly realised that if they couldn't speak to the schoolchildren this was going to be a hard report to run with.

"Is there any way around this though, because we really need to speak to them. Can you bring them in as a large group could that be done do you think?" Daniel looked to find out, and with that Max realised that this didn't sound like an idea that was entirely out of the question.

"I'll tell you what I'll do for you. I'll get a classroom organised for the schoolchildren that were witnesses along with the others that hadn't seen anything. That way nobody will feel too confronting with your questions?" Max wondered if this was something that would satisfy the UFO investigator and his assistant.

"That sounds like a good idea to me. What do you think Kelly does this make sense to you too?"

Daniel asked his secretary who gestured that this made complete sense to her, and with that they left the classroom and Max Davies behind them.

After having walked to the reception desk they looked at a face, which was kind of famous in UFO circles and it belonged to none other than noted UFO investigator Frederick Tate. He was there with his assistant Jennifer Lennon, and after a quick handshake they sought to speak with one another.

"You know each other then?" Mrs Pitman looked to find out if that indeed was the case - since they seemed friendly with one another.

"I wouldn't go that far, but I've been to a few seminars where Frederick Tate talked about his amazing missions tracking down UFO's." Daniel said to her, and Mrs Pitman looked on, as numerous schoolchildren were walking past them.

"I think that it might be for the best if you spoke in private, and that's not something that you'll be able to do if you stay here?" Mrs Pitman pointed out to them, and with that they left the school building in - order to speak in peace.

"So, what brings you here Frederick? Is it the same thing that brings us here by any chance? Have you also heard about the UFO, which was seen and witnessed by fourteen schoolchildren." Daniel sought to find out, and Frederick couldn't deny that was certainly the case since he hadn't come to Wales for a holiday in fact far from it.

"Yes. You've got me there, because both Jennifer and I heard about this case on the grapevine or whatever the UFO equivalent is. We realised that it was our duty to come to Broad Haven and check this out, because while they were only schoolchildren who witnessed this event that doesn't mean that they are automatically a poor judge of the sky. Not everyone has a vivid imagination, do they?" Frederick pointed out to them, and with that they headed out towards the car park.

"Where are you parked Frederick, because we could give you a lift towards our hotel. It's a nice one too, and I'm sure they'll be more than keen to have yourself and Jennifer staying there too?"

Kelly Evans suggested to Frederick who smiled before he answered the question.

"We've not yet booked into anywhere, because we didn't know how long we'd be staying here in Broad Haven. If you've got somewhere in mind, then that sounds like a plan to us?" Frederick informed Kelly and Daniel before they made the walk over towards the car.

"Are you parked close by too?" Kelly asked Jennifer who shook her head since they had parked at the railway station, because they hadn't yet booked into anywhere.

"No, we've got a bit of a walk unfortunately. Frederick was so excited by this sighting that he basically abandoned the car before we rushed to the school." Jennifer informed them moments before they got into Kelly's car, so that they could be given a lift to not only their car, but also to check into the Haven Fort Hotel.

Chapter Two

The Men in Black Arrive

On the outskirts of Wales another interested party was travelling in the company of two unnamed individuals, the six - foot eight - inch Man in Black known as Zodiac Isaac.

"Are you sure that this something worthy of our time Zodiac?" The man in the driver's looked to find out, but he just snarled back in his direction.

"Of course, because I've got a feeling that there is something about this specific UFO sighting." Zodiac informed them both although the man in the backseat of the car had something on his mind.

"From what I've heard this report was made by schoolchildren, and they are hardly the most rational people are they?" The man in the backseat wondered what Zodiac made of these accusations.

"Did you ever think that since they are school - children they wouldn't have made this incident up, because some children can be very reliable witnesses. Trust me I've been doing this job for some time, and I'm reserving judgement until we get to Broad Haven. I really think that you should feel the same way too, and when I say that - it's an order you have no other choice in the matter." Zodiac said to him, and with that the black coloured car became silent for a short period of time.

"Wales is a cold place to be at this time of the year, isn't it?" The man seated at the steering wheel looked to make some more pleasantries with Zodiac Isaac who nodded his head, as they noticed the sign for the town approaching them.

"Looks like we're almost there, but when we approach witnesses, I want you to follow my lead since I'm the lead investigator here." Zodiac Isaac advised them, as they continued - on the road to Broad Haven although having done so the rain started to lash down onto their car causing them to use the windscreen wipers.

"Typical Wales weather, eh?" The man seated in the backseat looked to gauge Zodiac Isaac's opinion on the subject, but he simply ignored him before looking out of the window of the passenger seat.

"Hey watch out!" Zodiac ordered the driver of the car to bring the car to a sudden stop, and he did that some moments later although was perplexed as to what was going on here.

"What's happening Zodiac? I mean why have we stopped?" The driver of the car sought to find out some specific details from the tall man in charge of this investigation.

"Wait here, because I'll be right back." Zodiac ordered him, and with that he got out of the car before using an umbrella in - order to flush someone or something out.

"What do you think he's up to out there?" The man in the backseat of the car asked the driver who wasn't sure what was happening since he hadn't seen anything.

"I've got a feeling that we'll soon find out. Zodiac isn't someone who suffers falls lightly and if he's out there then you can bet that it's for a good reason." The man in the driver's seat pointed out to him, as Zodiac looked behind a hedge where he soon discovered a man looking wet and dishevelled.

"Hello? What's your name and how did you come to be out here?" Zodiac was in search of answers, and one way or another this man was going to give them to him. The man took a deep breath, as he looked up at the hulking frame of the Man in Black.

"I've been feeling dizzy since yesterday, because I saw something quite amazing in the sky, and the worst of it is nobody believes me." The man informed Zodiac Isaac who himself had heard many a tale, so nothing was likely to shock the Man in Black.

"How about we give you a lift into Broad Haven, because this sounds like something the authorities need to hear about." Zodiac informed him before they rushed through the rain and on towards the waiting car with Zodiac's two associates located inside it.

"Hello? My name's Tomas Jones and you are?" Tomas asked the man seated beside him in the back of the car who just nodded his head back in his direction.

"This is my friend. We're undercover in a manner of speaking. We don't give out names to random people unfortunately." Zodiac announced to Tomas Jones who seemed to understand that this information wasn't something he needed to know here.

"What about the man driving the car, does he have a name or is he also undercover with no name to speak of?" Tomas suggested to Zodiac Isaac who smiled before lifting his hat that covered his head.

"He also is undercover, but you can talk to me instead - and trust me when I say that I've got more information than either of these two when it comes down to UFO's and things that roam around the sky." Zodiac explained to Tomas who after having heard this news seemed to relax in their company.

"I don't suppose you have a name yourself, do you?" Tomas wondered if it would be a case of third time lucky here and with that Zodiac had some information for him.

"My name is Zodiac Isaac, and I'm from a division of the MOD. I'm often sent here to look - into things that most people perhaps don't understand or more often don't want to deal with." Zodiac said to him moments before their car pulled up outside the police department with the rain tearing down on it.

"You two stay here. I'm going to go inside the police station with Tomas, because I've got a feeling that he probably needs a shoulder to lean on in a manner of speaking." Zodiac ordered his two associates before he got out of the car where he was closely followed by Tomas Jones.

Inside the police station Officer Daisy Campbell Edwards was on the front desk enjoying a quick cup of coffee along with a donut when she spied her visitors.

"Good evening gentlemen. What can I do for you this evening?" Officer Campbell Edwards sought to find out what they had on their minds and work out the reason why they were there this evening.

"My name's Tomas Jones, and I saw something spectacular in the sky earlier on. It was I believe something not of this world?" Tomas suggested to Daisy who laughed nervously before looking up at the giant Man in Black who didn't find anything amusing about this situation.

"Do you...did you also witness something weird in the sky sir?" Daisy sought to find out if that was the reason why Zodiac Isaac was also in attendance, but that wasn't it he was only there at this point as moral support.

"I didn't see anything on this occasion, but I've seen things before, so I know what Tomas is going through. Are you going to take some notes down or should I do that for you?" Zodiac quizzed Daisy who realised that she needed to be seen doing something, so she hollered over in the direction of her colleague Officer Rhys Dobson. He quickly made his way over towards the front desk in - order to find out what was going on since Daisy didn't normally signal for help unless she was genuinely concerned about something.

"What seems to be the issue here?" Officer Rhys Dobson asked both Zodiac Isaac and Tomas Jones who were pleased that he seemed to be open to their presence.

"Tomas here spotted something unusual in the sky, isn't that right Tomas?" Zodiac found himself speaking on behalf of the witness who nodded his head before he spoke for himself.

"That's right! I saw a UFO in the sky, and nothing anyone says can change that. I want you to log this into your system and investigate it, because that's something you need to do." Tomas informed them, and with that Daisy wrote the details down with her pen onto a pad of paper.

"Is there anything else or is that it?" Rhys wondered, but they didn't seem too impressed with his attitude feeling that something needed to be done here.

"Are you going to go near the Broad Haven School to check out this incident or not, because if you don't do it then I will along with my two colleagues?" Zodiac Isaac suggested to Rhys Dobson who recognised the school in question since his nephew was a student there.

"This is the same thing that happened to my nephew Douglas Dobson. He claimed that some people from another year saw UFO's or a UFO in the sky, but most people believe that they had to have been mistaken. Are you quite sure what you saw Tomas, it was really a UFO? I mean could it have been something you were mistaken about, because it could've been an aircraft from the local RAF- Station, couldn't it?" Rhys Dobson was obviously not getting carried away here and was grounded in - reality feeling that any UFO witness had to be treated with a heavy dose of scepticism.

"You said that your own nephew knew some people who also witnessed the UFO at the Broad Haven school? If that's the case, then how does he feel about the incident?" Zodiac Isaac suggested to the police officer, and he shrugged his shoulders in response.

"My nephew is twelve years old and has a big imagination. Plus, he is also a big fan of the BBC series Doctor Who, so obviously he wants to believe in science fiction." Officer Rhys Dobson pointed out to the giant Man in Black who was disappointed in his remarks.

"I can see that you aren't interested in following up these incidents or eyewitness reports. So, do you mind if we do it for you?" Zodiac Isaac wondered what he had to say about this idea, and by the looks of things he didn't mind in the slightest.

"Look if you want us to look - into it then we will, but not until tomorrow when the weather breaks again. It's not the best night out there something I'm sure you've noticed, and only Daisy and myself are currently on duty it will take more than the two of us to search around the area of the school." Officer Rhys Dobson informed him, and with that Zodiac thanked him for his time before walking away without Tomas Jones.

"Hey? You're leaving this man behind?" Daisy wondered what in the world was happening here, but he just raised his left arm in the air and continued walking away from them.

"I don't suppose I could trouble you for a cup of tea, could I? I've been soaked out there and then I'll make my own way home." Tomas informed Daisy who immediately beckoned him to follow her into the kitchen where she made him the cup of tea he'd asked for.

Zodiac Isaac got back into the black coloured car along with his two associates who'd got a couple of questions they wanted to have answered.

"What happened to that man? Did you lose him or dump him somewhere?" The man in the backseat of the car sought to find out where Tomas Jones was presently located, but Zodiac smiled.

"He's where he needs to be right now and that's with the police. I'm sure they'll get him home safely, but we've got a case to investigate here." Zodiac reminded them moments before he signalled for the man in the driver's seat to get them moving and away from the police station.

"Where are we off to now?" The man in the driver's seat sought to comply with his wishes since he needed to know what was going on.

"Bring this car to a stop!" Zodiac ordered the man behind the wheel who promptly complied with his wishes, and with that Zodiac jumped out of the car before making his way over towards two men who seemed to be knocking on doors.

"He's a bit strange sometimes, isn't he?" The man seated in the back of the car suggested to the driver who felt much the same way but wouldn't dare say this in case Zodiac overheard his comments.

"He's a good investigator though, and that's the main thing." The man in the driver's seat pointed out to him, as Zodiac walked up behind the two men in the street who were under two umbrellas.

"Excuse me gentlemen? I don't suppose you could tell me what you're doing, could you?" Zodiac wondered if they would be so good here, and with that they turned to look up at the hulking figure standing behind them.

"What can we do for you sir?" Roger Hammersley of the National geological survey sought to find out while his colleague Turner Hope was also intrigued to find out what this individual wanted from them.

"I don't suppose you could let me know the reasons behind you knocking on doors at this late hour of the day, because it seems somewhat out of place in the rain?" Zodiac Isaac hoped that they would let him know what was happening here, and with that Turner Hope nominated himself to speak on their behalf.

"We're here investigating an incident concerning a UFO. We have been asked to do this as part of our duties representing the National geological survey. What have you got to say to that?" Turner hoped that Zodiac Isaac would be equally as forthcoming with his answers.

"My name is Zodiac Isaac and along with my two companions, we have come here on behalf of the ministry of defence. We need to get to the bottom of what happened here, and just because most of the eyewitnesses to this event were children, we haven't been put off finding the underlining cause." Zodiac explained to the two men he was speaking with, and with that both Turner and Roger looked across at the black coloured car located not more than ten feet away from them.

"Don't look now, but I think we're being watched." The man in the back of the car pointed out to the driver who waved at Roger and Turner.

"You mean that there were other eyewitnesses as opposed to just schoolchildren, because we didn't know that until you said it." Turner informed Zodiac who didn't mind telling them this since it wasn't like they would be solving this investigation in his place.

"The man concerned was called Tomas Jones. My associates and I came across him earlier in the night and he was pretty - concerned that nobody would believe him. We took him to a police station where we made him make the report to an Officer Daisy Campbell Edwards and Officer Rhys Dobson." Zodiac explained to them, and they were pleased to hear it although they wanted to know where he was right now since they wanted to speak with him.

"Did you take him home, and do you have his address so that we might also be permitted to speak with him?" Roger suggested to Zodiac who swiftly shook his head to show that wouldn't be possible.

"We left him at the police station, we felt that would be the best thing for him right now. I don't think he was in any fit shape to be on his own right now." Zodiac informed them and with that they parted company with Zodiac making his way over towards the car, and the pair of people from the national geological survey continuing to knock on doors on this rain-filled night in Wales.

"Who were those people Zodiac and why were they waving at us?" The man seated in the back of the car was in search of some answers from his boss who felt that they had a right to know.

"They are from the national geological survey and have been sent here for the same reasons as we ourselves have been. To search for answers, as it relates to this UFO mystery, we find ourselves involved with." Zodiac said to them, and with that they sped away from the area in - order to take some shelter at a hotel situated in Broad Haven.

Frederick Tate and Jennifer Lennon had just stopped at the police station in - order to ask those on duty some questions, as it relates to directions around the area.

"Excuse me? Do you think we could ask you about something?" Frederick Tate asked Daisy Campbell Edwards who nodded her head to show that she was open to helping them out with their queries.

"What can we do for you?" Officer Daisy Campbell Edwards sought to find out what they had in mind here, and with that they were about to say what was on their minds when they noticed a man sleeping in a chair.

"Is that man quite alright?" Jennifer quizzed Daisy who nodded her head feeling that Tomas Jones was catching up on some well needed rest.

"Don't mind him. He came in here earlier on with a wide tale to tell, and he was accompanied by a tall man dressed entirely in black." Daisy explained to them, and while Jennifer didn't feel the need to ask for specific details Frederick certainly had to find out.

"What were those tales about, because I'm not adverse to certain tales myself in fact in my role as an investigator I'm more than used to it." Frederick said to Daisy who realised that she might as well tell him, because it wasn't like Tomas Jones would mind.

"He believes that he witnessed a UFO in the sky if you could simply imagine that? So, only he and a class full of fourteen – year - olds have seen this thing. I don't believe in anything like that myself, but what do you make of it considering you said that your used to wild tales?" Daisy suggested to Frederick Tate who smiled to himself, as he thought of the best way to respond to her question.

"I'm a full time UFO investigator and I'd like to tell you, that I'm here on holiday. Although if I did that then I'd just be lying to you. I've been a full - time investigator for about seven years now, and even had a bestselling book in nineteen seventy-four called 'The Newcastle Sighting'. A famous incident, which took place in North- East of England." Frederick said to Daisy just as Officer Rhys Dobson joined them in - order to see rather a shocked look on the face of his colleague.

"Are you quite alright Daisy?" Officer Dobson asked her, and with that she closed her mouth before turning to look at him.

"This is Frederick Tate and he's a UFO investigator. He's here, because of the UFO incident, which apparently took place at or near the Broad Haven school, isn't that right?" Daisy wondered if Frederick Tate would back her up here, and he didn't have an issue in doing that.

"That's right. I'm exactly what she said I am, a UFO investigator, so I'm here since word on the grapevine says you have something interesting to look - into." Frederick Tate announced to him, and with that the police seemed stunned, as if the news was sinking in for the first time.

"You know you are kind of making a believer out of me, and that's something that scares me to say." Officer Dobson informed them, and while Jennifer Lennon looked on Officer Daisy Campbell

Edwards provided some directions for them, that they'd initially walked into the station to get.

Chapter Three

The Morning After

The following morning Zodiac Isaac and his two colleagues left their guesthouse before making their way towards their black coloured car. The limped rainfall had subsequently given way to a scattering of winter sunshine, which lit up the puddles on both the pavement and the roads.

"This place looks different in the day - time, doesn't it?" The man seated behind the steering wheel sought to find out what his boss made of the current weather pattern.

"We've got a school to get to and with any luck there won't be anyone about the place at this time of the morning. I'm sorry I had to rush you both over breakfast, but time is of the essence, isn't it?" Zodiac suggested to them, and with that they powered away from their guesthouse before homing in on the Broad Haven School this early Saturday morning.

"I was just thinking something Zodiac, and you can shoot me down in flames in a manner of speaking of course. Surely there won't be anybody about the place all day today because it's Saturday, which doesn't require any teachers or students to attend the school?" The man seated in the back of the car hoped that his comments would be given a fair shake of the tree here, but that was never guaranteed with Zodiac Isaac about.

"I'm sure that there will still be someone in the building, and that's all we'll need to find out perhaps a caretaker or something." Zodiac said to them moments before they set off towards the school in - order to check this place out for themselves. After a short journey they arrived at the school gates only to find them locked, which wasn't a great surprise and even amused the man seated in the back of the car who predicted that this would happen.

"Come on let's get out of the car we've got something to check out." Zodiac ordered his two associates, and with that they followed his orders before making their way to the front gates. Zodiac's right hand lingered on the bell of the school, and then he pressed it. Just as predicted a man looked out of the window of the building where he realised that he had some visitors, and with that he cautiously made his way towards the front gates to see what they wanted this morning.

"Yes? Can I help you with something, because the school is closed, and the head of the school doesn't work on Saturday's." The caretaker Brinn Hughes pointed out to them, but they didn't have any interest in interacting with the head of the school they only had other things in mind.

"My name is Zodiac Isaac, and these are my two associates, and their names aren't important. We'd like to ask you a few questions about the UFO incident, which took place at this school yesterday. Do you think that we might be permitted to come in and take - a look around the grounds?" Zodiac hoped that he would go along with this request and with that Brinn Hughes feeling intimidated went along with his wishes.

"You are talking about the UFO a few of the schoolkids saw in the sky yesterday, aren't you?" Brinn suggested Zodiac, and the three men in black immediately nodded their heads in - order to show that he wasn't wrong on that score.

"Look I really shouldn't let you in, but I can see that you aren't the types of people who would take no for an answer?" Brinn wondered if he was reading the situation correctly, and Zodiac smiled back in his direction. Just before Zodiac and his two associates were allowed into the school building Jodie Rollings the newspaper writer arrived on the scene wanting to know what was happening here.

"Brinn, are you going to let these three strange looking men into the building? Are you sure that this would be a wise decision?" Jodie looked to find out what he had on his mind here, and with that Brinn appeared to be having second thoughts about his previous decision.

"How about you come into the building with us? Keep an eye on us, because we mean nobody any harm. Miss?" Zodiac suggested to her while hoping that she might introduce herself to them.

"My name is Jodie Rollings, and I work for the Broad Haven Star Newspaper. What about you who are you?" Jodie wondered if they would reciprocate and tell her who they happened to be.

"My name is Zodiac Isaac and I'm in charge of this investigation. My colleagues here and I are from a department from the ministry of defence. What do you know about the UFO, because I'm presuming that's the main reason why you are here today too?" Zodiac quizzed her, and with that Brinn Hughes motioned for everyone to follow him, because on this cold February morning it was kind of chilly outside. Once inside Brinn offered everyone a mug of tea, but not everyone took him up on the idea with only Jodie Rollings accepting his offer.

"Do you know whereabouts the schoolkids were yesterday when they spied the UFO?" Zodiac asked Brinn who nodded his head before leading this group of individuals out of the building and into the playground.

"I believe that it was up in the sky, way up there?" Brinn announced before pointing with his right arm up in the air although the sky seemed to be cloudy and clear right now.

"Get your camera out, because we still need to take some stills of the sky. Things need to be documented here." Zodiac ordered his driver who took out a camera in - order to take the stills that the large Man in Black wanted.

"What are they doing taking pictures of a blank sky, because it makes next to no sense to me. As a reporter I'm asking you since I thought you might know the answer to my question?" Brinn looked at Jodie Rollings who understood where he was coming from.

"Hopefully they will leave the place once they've got their pictures developed. There is something about them, that worries and concerns me." Jodie announced her feelings on Zodiac Isaac and his two associates who were still discussing things a few hundred metres away from them. They then turned and looked at Brinn Hughes and Jodie Rollings before they made their way back over towards them clearly having something on their minds.

"Thank you for your hospitality. My associates and I will now leave you in peace, but we'll be back on Monday where we fully on speaking with several witnesses and the headteacher of this school." Zodiac informed Brinn and Jodie before the startled pair watched on, as the Men in Black marched their way into the main building to leave the school behind.

"They are going to quiz the schoolkids, because that's what they meant by those remarks isn't it, Jodie?" Brinn suggested to the reporter from the Broad Haven Star who was concerned by the comments about interviewing the schoolkids.

"By the sounds of things, but don't worry Brinn as - long as I'm around I'm going to make sure that doesn't take place. I don't think I've ever met such strange looking gentlemen before." Jodie informed him, but just as she was leaving another couple of people turned up on the scene.

"Hello? My name's Frederick Tate and this is my assistant Jennifer Lennon. We've come here to speak to you about the UFO that was witnessed yesterday?" Frederick announced to them, and with that Brinn looked somewhat out of sorts, as this kind of thing was developing into a habit.

"My name's Jodie Rollings and I believe we spoke to each other on the phone yesterday. I've just come out of the school where I can tell you for nothing that there's simply nothing to see. The sky is presently empty just a few winter's clouds to be seen on the horizon." Jodie explained to them in the hopes of disparaging them into wanting to access the Broad Haven School building.

"It's a pleasure to meet you again, Jodie. Do you happen to work in the school as well or are you merely visiting?" Frederick wanted some details from her, and Jodie realised that it might be for the best if she divulged where she worked.

"I just have one job as a reporter for the Broad Haven Star. I'm also really interested in this story, but after we'd spoken to three strange men, we feel that a strange tale has become somewhat stranger?" Jodie informed the pair of people who'd come to look at the sight of where the UFO incident had taken place.

"What do you mean by three strange men?" Jennifer Lennon sought to find out about these people since her mind was now running away with her.

"Yes. There was one man who introduced himself to us. His name I believe was Zodiac Isaac and he was with two people he didn't share their names with us just called them his colleagues." Jodie explained to them, and with that a worrying thought ran through the mind of Frederick Tate since he knew all about Zodiac Isaac the Man in Black.

"Do you know what they were doing while they were here, and more importantly where they went when they left the school?" Frederick was now in search of urgent answers, and his reaction made Brinn Hughes and Jodie Rollings feel concerned.

"You know who those people are? Are they dangerous?" Brinn Hughes suggested to Frederick Tate who wasn't really - sure the best way to answer his question since while they were Men in Black they seemed to be on the good side of things.

"We've met them a few times before, and if they've shown up then there has - to be a good reason for it. You haven't let them near the eyewitnesses yet, have you?" Frederick wondered while feeling that letting the Men in Black loose could be concerning for any witness.

"They were children. Fourteen of them to be precise, and no it's Saturday so the children weren't at school today. We're kind of hoping that the three men won't come back on Monday, but they didn't seem to be too bothered and took pictures of the sky on a camera." Jodie explained to Jennifer and Frederick who looked up into the darkening Winter sky, which looked like it was due to rain again at any moment.

"What was in the sky at the time?" Jennifer looked to find out what they'd captured since it was kind of odd behaviour to take pictures of a blank sky.

"Nothing, that's the problem. Do you want to go a café to get something to eat and drink, because I could do with something about now." Jodie said to Frederick Tate and Jennifer Lennon who felt that now would be as good as time as ever to get something to eat. Brinn Hughes immediately bolted the front gates of the school building in - order to ensure nobody else got into the place, well at least while he was around.

Daniel Price and Kelly Evans were in the café eating something when Frederick Tate walked in with Jennifer Lennon and Jodie Rollings.

"Hey, look who it is? It's only Frederick Tate." Daniel pointed out to Kelly who looked up from her bowl of tomato soup to see the man and his party taking a seat near the window booth.

"You'll need to go over there and introduce yourself, don't you or do you want me to do it for you?" Kelly wondered what picture frame he wanted to have picked for him here, and with that Daniel took a deep breath before he got up and slowly made his way over towards Frederick Tate, Jennifer Lennon and Jodie Rollings.

"Hello? You don't know me, but my name is Daniel Price and I'm here today with my secretary Kelly Evans. She's sitting right over there. Anyhow, I'm a UFO investigator just like you

Frederick Tate. It's an honour to meet you today. Have you been to the school yet?" Daniel asked them in - order to see if they would be willing to share some information with him since he hadn't made the kind of progress, he'd previously hoped he would.

"Did you go to the school today?" Jennifer Lennon suggested to him, and with that they were given the once over by Kelly Evans who nominated herself to speak on their behalf.

"No. We went there yesterday where we spoke to a few teachers and a school secretary, but they didn't exactly make us feel welcome." Kelly informed them before they took up a couple of chairs next to Jodie Rollings who thought now would be a good time to let this pair know about the mysterious people who showed up today.

"I think now is the time don't you Frederick?" Jodie suggested to him, and with that he puffed out his cheeks before taking a deep breath.

"It would seem, that we aren't alone in wanting to get to the bottom of this mystery, because the Men in Black are also in town. Trust me when I say you have - to be careful when they are around, and if they are here then they truly believe a UFO has landed in Broad Haven." Frederick pointed out to them moments before the bell on the door went and in walked the two people from the natural geological survey Roger Hammersley and Turner Hope.

"Two cups of coffee please." Roger said to the waitress Louise Brown who wanted to know where they were going to be seated, and with that they pointed to the booth next to Frederick Tate and company.

"Have you spoken to them two yet?" Daniel suggested to Frederick who wasn't sure why he would need to consult with these two gentlemen.

"Who are they then?" Frederick wondered what the reason was here, and with that Daniel sought to let him know the reasons why.

"They are here to do much the same thing we're here for, but they represent the National geological survey." Daniel announced to Frederick who immediately waved over the two men concerned, they approached the table to see what he wanted from them.

"Hello? It's nice to see you again Daniel and Kelly, but you're going to have to introduce us to the rest of your friends?" Turner Hope wondered if he would be so good, and with that he nodded his head.

"This is Jodie Rollings from the local newspaper. It also gives me a great deal of pleasure to introduce you to Frederick Tate the noted UFO investigator along with his assistant Jennifer Lennon." Daniel explained to them, and with that they shook hands with everyone at the table.

"Frederick Tate, I don't remember us ever meeting before, but it's obvious that we are both here to investigate what's really happening in Broad Haven. I suppose you expect little green men to appear and turn up at any moment?" Roger Hammersley suggested to the startled UFO investigator who felt that these accusations were slightly unfair.

"I'm not going to lie to you, but things tend to turn up around a UFO event and not everything is a laughing matter." Frederick said to them clearly in a defensive manner, and with that the pair from the National geological survey took their leave where they received their coffees from the waitress Louise Brown.

"I'm sorry you had to hear that Frederick, because not everyone around Broad Haven feels the same way as they do." Daniel shared his take on proceedings with the more experienced man seated opposite him.

"It's okay. Everyone is entitled to an opinion whether we agree with it or not, but if something happens to one of those people or Lord forbid the pair of them. Well, someone will have to come to their rescue and that someone could well be sitting at this table." Frederick pointed out to an alarmed looking Daniel Price, who hadn't up to now even contemplated the idea that they would potentially have to fight with the Alien menace should it show up here.

"Forgive my asking Jennifer and Frederick, but in the event of something showing up looking for a fight from another world? How would we go about defeating them?" Kelly Evans was on serious alert here since she hadn't given this idea a second thought when she'd come to Broad Haven with Daniel Price.

"Well, I'm not too sure to be honest. I'm kind of hoping the art of dialect and diplomacy isn't dead and we might be capable of asking them politely to leave the place." Frederick informed Kelly who wasn't exactly getting carried away with this idea since the idea of coming face – to – face with an Alien now loomed large in her mind.

The bell on the door went again and in walked someone that looked like he was in a serious need of a caffeine boost.

"Hello Tomas? Are you feeling okay, because you look somewhat lost in the moment for some strange reason?" Louise Brown greeted Tomas Jones the man who'd not only seen the UFO yesterday but had also been in the company of the Men in Black.

"Yes. A strong mug of tea thanks Louise. I need some kind of boost here after the past few hours. You'll never believe what happened to me yesterday and it's not something I'm so sure about myself." Tomas admitted to her without elaborating on what he was talking about, and this caused Louise to feel intrigued, so she wanted to find out exactly what he was on about.

"What happened to you then, you know yesterday?" Louise suggested to him before passing him the hot mug of tea he'd come in there for.

"I saw a UFO and before you start laughing at me? I'm being about as serious as I've ever been about this. Then I got lost in the rain last night where I was picked out of the rain by a tall man, and together with his colleagues we got taken to the police station. I was in a bad way though, and I'm only just kind of recovering from it now." Tomas said to her and with that Frederick Tate hollered over in his direction in - order to get his attention.

"Looks like someone is pleased to see you?" Louise suggested to Tomas who reluctantly made his way over towards the booth to speak with Frederick Tate and company.

"I don't suppose you know who that is do you, because it would help me enormously if I was to know who I'm dealing with?" Tomas wondered if

Louise could supply this very important piece of information his way.

"All I know is that they have been talking about UFO's so if you ask me then you will probably be in your element, won't you?" Louise said to him, and with that Tomas made his way over towards Frederick Tate and company before sitting down on the chair they'd pulled up for him.

"I don't believe we've met before, but my assistant Jennifer and I saw you while you were asleep in the police station last night. What were you doing there if we don't mind my asking?" Frederick Tate asked him, and Tomas wasn't ashamed to admit that he'd been lost while searching for answers following his UFO sighting.

"I was there reporting my UFO sighting in the day. I saw something, which shouldn't have been there, and I felt like someone should know about it." Tomas explained to them, and with that Daniel was intrigued and hoped that he might be able to ask him a question.

"Do you mind if I ask a question Frederick?" Daniel wondered and Frederick nodded his head in - order to show that he didn't have an issue with his doing that.

"What do you want from me?" Tomas looked to find out what he had on his mind here and with that Daniel immediately came out with his question.

"Were you close to the school when you saw the UFO, because we found out that fourteen schoolchildren saw the UFO in the sky while they had been in the playground. Were you close by too?" Daniel suggested to him, and with that Tomas took a few sips of his strong mug of tea as he contemplated his response.

"I was actually - walking past the school when I saw the blasted thing. I wish I'd taken a photograph of the UFO that way nobody would doubt what I had to say about it. You know the police weren't interested in it, and the only people who were – were the three men in black suits who took me to the police station. Although they disappeared while I was inside, and I don't know what happened to them?" Tomas explained to them, and Frederick immediately knew who they were, because it was Zodiac Isaac and his two associates who for some reason didn't have names at least not that he knew of.

"Three men in black suits? You know who that is don't you Frederick?" Jennifer looked for a positive response to her question and with that Frederick took a deep sounding sigh.

"I don't suppose you've seen them since your release, have you?" Frederick suggested to Tomas who shook his head since he'd already stated that they'd disappeared after they'd dropped him off.

"No. Also, between the two of us I don't mind not seeing them again. They kind of gave me the creeps." Tomas admitted to the people who sat around the table, but they just looked concerned about what the Men in Black might be doing next.

"I believe that we'll probably run into them sooner or later, because that's just the way the things seem to go." Frederick said to them, but some moments later in walked Zodiac Isaac and his two associates who immediately made their way over towards the world - renowned UFO investigator.

"Well – well Frederick Tate. I'd wonder what you are doing here in Broad Haven at this precise point in time, but I've got a feeling that I already know the answer to that particular - question." Zodiac informed him, and with that Frederick looked upwards at the towering member of the Men in Black.

"How did you find out yourself about this UFO, Zodiac?" Frederick knew that this was a question he probably wouldn't answer - but felt compelled to ask him the question all the same.

"You should know me well enough by now Mister Tate. You know that we are from the government department, which doesn't answer to any members of the general - public. I'm not meaning to sound condescending in any way, but you are at the end of the day a member of that very same general - public." Zodiac pointed out to him before he sat down at a table across the café from the noted UFO investigator.

"How do you know that man Zodiac?" The man seated to his right -hand side looked to find out since he hadn't mentioned him until he met him.

"Let's just say that we need to find that UFO before he does or otherwise, he'll end up writing a book about it or something along those lines and drawing attention to the fact that something major happened here. It's just not something our department wants to see happen don't you agree with me?" Zodiac suggested to his colleague who understood the point he was trying to make - but felt that they needed to find out what this thing was before they wrote it off as a simple UFO incident.

"What I want to know is whether or not you think that this UFO is just an object or if it's intelligently operated?" The man seated to his left – hand side wondered where he stood on this idea.

"You are talking about Aliens, aren't you?" Zodiac understood where he was going here and felt that this was what it amounted up to.

"That's what I was getting at, and I'm all ears for your views on this since I've never seen an Alien in person myself. Have you Zodiac?" The man hoped to get his inside views on this one and with that Zodiac had a wry chuckle to himself before he spoke his mind.

"You are seriously asking your commanding officer if he's seen an alien before?" Zodiac sought for the man to clarify his comments, and the man reiterated what he'd just said causing Zodiac to smirk.

"I've seen more than a few strange things since I've been involved in this job and before you two were assigned to my unit, I've come across numerous alien beings even spoke to them and got them to agree to leaving the place they sought to takeover. Now I don't know what's behind this incident yet, but if it is indeed Aliens then you can stand behind me and I'll talk to the beings concerned. They might see sense before we need to take urgent action and trust me if they are indeed hostile then it won't be for the faint hearted." Zodiac explained to them just as their food orders and drinks arrived at the table although the man sat to his right – hand side had something urgent on his mind.

"What happens if that man Frederick Tate and his friends get there, before we do? I mean wouldn't that kind of complicate the situation and there's no telling if he'll get on the bad side of these beings, is there?" The man suggested to Zodiac who couldn't deny that he'd come up with a sensible question at least on this specific occasion.

"We'll just have to hope that occasion doesn't exist - or else things could get complicated and possibly messy along with it. You two aren't afraid of getting your hands dirty, are you?" Zodiac wondered where they stood on this idea, and with that they fell somewhat silent as they contemplated what he'd just said to them.

"We'll be there right beside you Zodiac. That's something that you can indeed rely on. That's our job and our duty too." The man seated to his left – hand side showed that he had their backing here and that made Zodiac feel a lot more at ease at their company.

"That's exactly what I wanted to hear." Zodiac said to them before they looked up, as Frederick Tate and company left the café behind them, as they sought to get to the bottom of this mystery.

Frederick Tate and Jennifer Lennon were walking down the lanes along with Daniel Price and Kelly Evans who were equally as enthusiastic as solving this mystery as they were.

"That was one of the biggest men I've ever seen in my life." Kelly Evans admitted to being surprised at the height of the six – foot – eight - inch Man in Black called Zodiac Isaac.

"You've been fairly - quiet Frederick, which isn't like you. Have you got a lot on your mind?" Jennifer Lennon sought to find out what he was presently thinking and with that Frederick stopped walking before he turned around to face them.

"I've met that man Zodiac Isaac many times over the years, well ever since nineteen – seventy – four. Newcastle was my first introduction to Zodiac Isaac and to be honest with you I'm not so sure he's even a human being." Frederick was honest with them and shared his current state of mind with them.

"I know that this is going to sound quite odd, but I've come to the shocking conclusion that the tallest member of the Men in Black isn't human at all." Frederick pointed out to them, and with that Daniel Price looked shaken up at his comments while Jennifer Lennon watched on in silence.

"If this...well individual isn't human then what is he then?" Kelly Evans hoped that he wouldn't be backwards in coming forwards here, and with that Frederick took a couple of deep breaths before he shared his mind with them.

"I happen to believe that he's some kind of alien himself. I don't know what planet he comes from, but my parents always used to tell me to be aware of people you meet who never seem to age. Just like Zodiac Isaac?" Frederick suggested to them, and with that Jennifer Lennon found her voice once more whereupon she was looking to get her question answered.

"That might all be down to good genes though, don't you agree with me?" Jennifer asked him, and with that he shook his head back in her direction to show that he thought that Zodiac's appearance had something more to do with being an alien life form.

"I think that for the time – being we should perhaps reserve judgement on that idea, because I don't know how anybody else feels about things, but the notion that I've just met an alien being is giving me some serious chills." Daniel Price hoped that he wasn't the only one that felt that way and some moments later a woman rushed up to them with something on her mind.

"Are you the UFO people who've come to town to search for the aliens?" She asked them in hopeful fashion, and with that Frederick felt all eyes suddenly beam around him and he realised that he needed to be the one to address her comments.

"We've come to town to find what's been causing the commotion, we can't deny that's the truth. What's your involvement in this incident?" Frederick hoped that she wouldn't be backwards in coming forwards here, and with that she looked around where there seemed to be nobody about and the roads were equally as quiet.

"I saw it land somewhere close to the school. I don't know how many others saw this happen, so I feel that my observation is worth considering.

My name's Joanna Reader by the way." Joanna shared some key details with them and with that they felt that it would be for the best if she showed them where the UFO landed, because that way they would be able to see if the UFO left any marks on the ground.

"It's nice to meet you, Joanna Reader. My name name's Frederick Tate, this is my assistant Jennifer Lennon. These are our new associates Daniel Price and Kelly Evans." Frederick announced to her and then they shook hands with one another before they started following Joanna Reader on towards where she believed the UFO had landed.

"How long have you been sitting on this information Joanna?" Daniel Price was looking to find out if she'd spoken to anyone else about this place, but she just looked at him before shaking her head.

"You are the first people I've told this to. I got your details from a friend of mine who works in the café, because she felt that I could trust you. I was also given details about three mysterious people wearing black business suits, but the very idea of them made me feel like they weren't going to be the best people to approach." Joanna said to them, and with that they continued back towards the area around the school where Joanna had made her sighting.

Zodiac Isaac and company had meanwhile decided to check out another area of the beach where they felt that the UFO had possibly submerged.

"Are you really - sure that this is a proper UFO, Zodiac? I mean if it goes underwater then it has got to be a submarine?" The man stood to his left – hand wondered what he made of his remarks, which judging from the expression on his face wasn't a great deal.

"You need to know what we're dealing with. UFO'S don't always just land on the ground, because sometimes they go under the water too. Not just submarines that's something you need to learn and keep in mind from this moment onwards." Zodiac Isaac shared some insight with him, and he seemed happy enough to take his words onboard.

"Do you think that the UFO is possibly underwater then?" The man stood to his right – hand side sought to find out what he made of the idea.

"I've had a quick scan, and I can't see that it's underwater. So, while we need to keep things like this in mind. I'm hoping that this UFO and its inhabitants come back once more, so that we can capture them." Zodiac Isaac informed them, and in doing so did more than a little alarm them too since he'd never mentioned the word capture before.

"When you say capture them?" The man to his left – hand side wondered if he would be so good as to clarify his remarks for them.

"I'm just talking about the worse - case scenario here. I'm sure that they won't be too hostile once we do come across them, well if we do that's an open question that might not be answered right now." Zodiac said to them, and with that they made their way back over towards their parked black – coloured car which was located on the beach front.

"Not too much traffic about around here, is there?" The man walking to his right – hand side pointed out the obvious to Zodiac who puffed his cheeks out before sighing for him to have stated the obvious.

"You ever think that's because that we are a little out of season here? I mean when you come to think about it who wants to come to a Welsh seaside resort during a cold winter's season?" Zodiac suggested to them and with that they got into their car before making the journey back towards the school where they intended to get some more insight into what'd happened.

"I know that you aren't going to like this Zodiac?" The man driving the car sought to get his remarks, and with that the man leading this mission realised that he needed to answer his question, which was hanging in the air.

"What aren't I going to like then. Please do enlighten me?" Zodiac Isaac hoped that this would be an easy thing to do here, and with that the man driving the car shared his feelings with him.

"What happens if Frederick Tate and his merry band of men and women find the UFO and perhaps some occupants before we do. Would the aliens turn hostile on them?" The man wondered what the tall Man in Black made of the notion and with that he looked up as they arrived back at the school once more.

"In that case we will just have to hope they don't find them first, because not everyone has - the ability to communicate with these beings. Not everyone will get through to their good side, because they haven't been trained." Zodiac Isaac explained to them before they got out of their car and made their way down towards the school gates.

"Hello? How long have you been here?" Zodiac sought to take some details from a pair of people he'd come across before, and he hoped that they wouldn't keep their identities to themselves in the daylight.

"Not for too long. I believe we've met each other before. My name's Roger Hammersley and this is my colleague Turner Hope we are from the National Geological Survey. We are following up reports about a UFO incident, I don't suppose you well – dressed gentlemen have seen anything yourselves?" Roger suggested to Zodiac who while he didn't know who they were personally had certainly heard of the National Geological Survey.

"Follow my lead here." Zodiac ordered his two associates who didn't have a problem doing that and just nodded their heads to show they would do that.

"Have we seen anything since we've been in Broad Haven? Nothing science fiction let's just put it that way. Now you've asked me. What about you have you seen anything yourselves?" Zodiac hoped that Turner Hope and Roger Hammersley would be equally open in sharing their current findings.

"Unfortunately, we've yet to find an alien being running around the streets of Broad Haven, and perhaps that's for the best. We've been in town for a day or so now and we've interviewed numerous people, but for the most part it's been hearsay." Turner Hope informed the giant Man in

Black who nodded his head, as he took his comments on board.

"Are you also going into the school, because we've found to our disappointment that there isn't a great deal to be uncovered there especially not at this time of the day?" Zodiac suggested to Roger and Turner who looked at each other before looking back in his direction.

"Are you saying that there aren't any staff about?" Turner wondered if he was guessing correctly here, and with that they looked on, as Brinn Hughes opened the school gates before he approached them to see what they wanted.

"You three again? What do you need from me today?" Brinn sought to find out what Zodiac Isaac and his colleagues had on their minds.

"We found out that the UFO was also seen by other witnesses, so we were going to look for access to the lanes around the school. If that's okay with you?" Zodiac hoped that Brinn would be helpful to their cause here, and with that Brinn nodded his head while indicating that shouldn't be an issue.

"I don't have a problem with that providing of course you take care of the property and don't do any damage." Brinn pointed out to Zodiac who snarled back in his direction before he entered the school once more along with his two associates.

"Can we enter too?" Turner Hope sought to find out and with that Brinn Hughes gestured for the two men from the National geographical society.

"Well, I can't let them in without you entering too." Brinn advised them, and with that Roger Hammersley and Turner Hope followed him into the main area of the school building.

"Do you think that you could perhaps show us around?" Turner suggested to Brinn who didn't have an issue in doing that, and with that they followed him out into the school playground where they noticed that the Men in black had already disappeared elsewhere and were no longer in view.

"Have you met that man before, what did you think of him since he came off as being somewhat odd?" Roger Hammersley suggested to Brinn who nodded his head to show he understood where he was coming from.

"I'm glad that I'm not the only one who feels the same way about the tall person. He seems to be somewhat suited to investigating UFO's." Brinn informed the pair of them before they noted some comments down onto their pair of clipboards.

"I don't think that there's any particular person that would fit looking into UFOS, because we do - and we'd like to think of ourselves as normal most of the time." Turner Hope said to Brinn Hughes who understood where he was coming from.

Meanwhile Frederick Tate, Jennifer Lennon, Daniel Price and Kelly Evans were busy speaking to numerous people over the other side of Broad Haven in – order to see just how many people had seen the UFO - but hadn't yet stepped forward to register the fact.

"So, you saw the UFO, did you?" Frederick asked Alice Nelson who nodded her head to show that she'd certainly seen something that she couldn't explain.

"That's right I saw it all right. It appeared in the sky while I was riding home on my bicycle, and I was so distracted that I nearly came off the bike. It was only there for a short while however, and it left me with more questions than answers. Do you know what it is I saw in the sky?" Alice said to them, and with that all – eyes turned to Frederick in – order to see if he'd got an explanation for her.

"Not yet, but we're working on it. Did you happen to see anything on the ground since sometimes these things do land too?" Frederick suggested to her and with that Alice shook her head to show that she'd not seen anything - or anyone connected with the UFO following the initial sighting.

"No, I'm sorry although having said that I'm not sorry since the last thing I want to come across is an alien being right here in Broad Haven." Alice explained to him just as they were joined by another UFO witness and her good friend Joanna Reader.

"Are you okay Alice? What's going on here?" Amie Charles immediately leapt to the defence of her friend while hoping that someone might be able to bring her up to speed.

"We're here investigating the UFO sighting. My name's Frederick Tate, this is my assistant Jennifer Lennon, and these are our new friends Daniel Price and Kelly Evans?" Frederick Tate suggested to Amie Charles who realised that they were there to help not bother her friend.

"It's good to see you here in person and you all want to know what I witnessed while I'd been driving home in my car?" Amie sought to find out if she was reading the situation correctly and with that, they all made their way towards the beach to continue speaking.

"Did you see the UFO for any duration of time or was it sighted then gone in a flash?" Frederick Tate wondered how long the sighting lasted for and with that Amie and Alice both nodded their heads before Amie spoke.

"I saw it for what seemed like a few minutes, but it could've been longer or less than that. I'd estimate a few minutes, but didn't look at my watch for confirmation of the fact." Amie said to them while Frederick and Jennifer took down her comments.

Chapter Four

Night Arrives

Sometime later - on the night had arrived in Broad Haven and Zodiac Isaac along with his two associates were driving around in their black coloured car when they decided to enter the police station on the off chance that something else might've been reported.

"Heads – up, looks who's coming our way." Officer Rhys Dobson said to his colleague Officer Daisy Campbell-Edwards who was concerned about the idea of seeing Zodiac Isaac back inside their police station.

"Good evening to you both. My colleagues and I are here to enquire about how much you've found out about the UFO we were interested in yesterday." Zodiac Isaac asked them in confident manner and with that the police looked at each other before looking back in his direction again.

"We asked our colleagues who do the daytime shift, but they didn't make much progress I'm afraid. It would seem as if your mysterious object has pulled a disappearing trick on us all." Officer Rhys Dobson announced to a visibly disappointed looking Zodiac Isaac who breathed a huge sigh of deflation.

"The police aren't doing their jobs properly." Zodiac called out to his two colleagues who were stood behind him with their arms folded in defensive fashion.

"If they haven't made any progress then what happens now?" The man stood to his left – hand side sought to find out what he'd got on his mind here, but moments later the desk phone of the police started ringing. Officer Daisy Campbell-Edwards picked up moments later grateful for the distraction if nothing else here.

"Hello, police department Broad Haven?" She sought to find out what the call was about and moments later she did.

"Good evening. My name's Owen Meridith and I'm a farmer at a property located not that far away from you. My family and I have just had a visitation." Owen informed a startled looking Daisy who tentatively found herself repeating the information back to him.

"You've had a visitation you say? Could I enquire as to who that was?" Daisy sought to find out while her colleague Officer Rhys Dobson, Zodiac Isaac and his two colleagues looked on with much intrigue.

"I don't know who it was, but it's unusual for my farmhouse to be visited on a dark winter's evening by someone dressed in black looking in through my window." Owen explained to Daisy who hurriedly wrote the information down as she looked concerned.

"How long was the visitor there for and what did you do to make him or her disappear again?" Daisy asked some important questions, and ones that Owen thought made a lot of sense.

"Initially we were all scared, but then I picked up my shotgun before aiming it at the window. The figure clad - entirely in black took one look at it before they disappeared almost like they'd never been there." Owen pointed out to Daisy who then took down his address and promising to interview him at his farmhouse in around half an hour's time.

"What's happened, because this sounds like something my colleagues and I should get involved in here." Zodiac Isaac thought all things considered this sounded like the way ahead.

"I really don't - know? Rhys, do you think that they'd be able to help us out or should we just travel ourselves to the farmhouse?" Daisy thought all things considered her colleague who'd been working for the police for a few years longer than her should have the final say.

"I can see that the gentlemen in our presence could be of some help to us, so with our blessing you can come with us. Having said that you need to leave it to us when it comes to the important questions." Officer Dobson pointed out to Zodiac Isaac who nodded his head to show that he'd take their comments on board, but whether - or not he'd listen to them was another thing entirely.

"We'll follow your lead." Zodiac said to them, but in doing so caught the attention of both his colleagues as they sought to leave the police station for the car park.

"Are we really going to leave it to them, because now we have the address, we can just go there without them?" The man situated to his left-hand side thought that they were giving the police the edge when it came to the investigation.

"Don't worry, because when the time comes to question this man Owen Meridith we'll get to the bottom of things while the police are just asking the most basic things. It's what they usually do when it comes to UFO investigations - and trust me I know what I'm talking about here." Zodiac Isaac confirmed for them both as they followed the police vehicle in their black coloured car to the address of Owen Meridith.

Owen Meridith was seated in his living room patiently waiting for the police to arrive while he'd already sent his family up to bed feeling that was probably for the best. Although he was still on edge, and had his trusty shotgun situated close to hand. Some moments later his wife walked into the room looking weary and concerned.

"I thought that you were going to bed?" Owen suggested to her while feeling that was most probably for the best, but she shook her head back in his direction.

"How could I sleep after all we've seen tonight. You've got to admit that it's not every-day we see a figure at our window at this hour of the night?" Nerys Meridith pointed out to her husband before she sat down next to him on the sofa, but moments later the doorbell went, and Owen gestured for her to remain still.

"Good evening? Are you the one I spoke to on the telephone?" Owen sought to find out from Officer Daisy Campbell-Edwards who shook his hand before confirming that she was indeed one in the same.

"Yes. I'm Daisy and this is my colleague Officer Rhys Dobson along with our three specialists in this line of field." Daisy said to him and with that he brought them all into his living room where they greeted his wife.

"This is my wife, Nerys. These are the people who are here to help us answer the questions we need to find the answers to." Owen informed his wife who seemed pleased to have them in her living room.

"Now I'd like you to take us back to the sighting itself. Did you happen to witness anything in the sky outside before you noticed the figure at your window?" Officer Daisy Campbell-Edwards suggested to Owen who understood the nature of the question.

"No, well nothing other than the moon of course. What was there to see in the sky?" Owen suggested to them and with that Zodiac Isaac stepped forward to let him know what they were referring to.

"There have been recent reports about UFO's hanging around the town of Broad Haven. Obviously, the fact that you've seen a figure hanging around outside your window we kind of had the feeling that it might've been an alien being. What do you make of that?" Zodiac wondered and with that Owen turned away from them before he walked over towards the window where he looked outside, but only sighted the moon out there.

"I never noticed anything of such description today or yesterday for that matter. I didn't know anything about UFO's being seen in Broad Haven before you just shared that information with me. Are you telling me that you think that I've been visited by a real - life alien?" Owen thought all things considered this still sounded like a bit of a stretch and with that he turned back towards the towering Man in Black who nodded his head.

"That's correct. How did you get rid of this individual who appeared at your window? I take it you didn't converse with him?" Zodiac thought that a lack of dialogue was more than a real possibility here.

"That's right. I approached my window with my shotgun cocked and loaded, and when I aimed it at the induvial it disappeared like it'd never even been there in the first place. It was there though, because my entire family had seen it." Owen explained to them and with that his wife placed a comforting arm around his shoulder.

"We won't reach for the conclusion that you've actually seen an alien being, because the chances are that's not what it was." Zodiac Isaac was somewhat dismissive about their chances of having witnessed someone from another world.

"Then what did I see in that case?" Owen wondered if anyone could step forwards and share some more information with him.

"The chances are it was just young people being bored and playing pranks on local people. Taking their chances of scaring those that had heard about the UFO's earlier on yesterday." Officer Rhys Dobson found himself being the voice of reason here and with that the police along with the Men in Black sought to leave the property behind.

Zodiac Isaac and his two associates made their way over towards the window outside the farmhouse living room where Zodiac shone a torch over the soil located there.

"What's going on Zodiac, what can you see?" The man situated to his right – hand side wondered if he'd gone and solved this mystery.

"Looks like size nine shoes to me. One thing about aliens in my experience, and that's the fact they don't go shopping at the same places as human beings. These tracks weren't made by beings from another world, and whoever left them here was lucky farmer Owen Meridith didn't shoot them. It would've been a bit of a high price just for the sake of a prank." Zodiac informed them before he walked back over towards their black coloured car whereupon they drove off towards their guest house where they'd spend the rest of the evening. Meanwhile in the police patrol car Officer Daisy Campbell-Edwards and Officer Rhys Dobson were considering their part in the investigation and thought all things considered they didn't have much to be too concerned about.

"Well, that went well with the farmer and his wife. They were suitably relaxed after we shared our findings with them when it comes to the footprints outside the window." Officer Daisy

Campbell-Edwards said to her colleague who nodded his head.

"That's right. I was alarmed before we got there - I'm not going to lie about that, but when those Men in Black found those human footprints, it calmed my nerves. They were racing before that since the last thing we needed was to find something not of this world. I mean what language would be communicate in. because it's not guaranteed we could converse in English?" Officer Dobson suggested to her before the pair of them laughed in relieved fashion.

"How do we go about finding those responsible though, that's the thing that we must think about doing?" Officer Campbell-Edwards thought that they couldn't close the book on this just yet.

"I don't know since I'm thinking that having a shotgun pulled on you while you're in the middle of a prank might be punishment enough. I can't imagine anyone stepping forward when we advertise this crime and saying that they were responsible." Officer Dobson said to her, as they pulled up to the police station where they found

Frederick Tate and Jennifer Lennon situated there.

"Heads-up, here we go again?" Officer Campbell-Edwards suggested to her colleague as they exited the car and made their way over towards the two people from the UFO investigation.

"Good evening to the pair of you. How can we help you today?" Officer Rhys Dobson sought to find out what had brought them there this evening, and they wouldn't have to wait around too long to find out.

"We've come across a couple of people dressed in black - clothing and they threw these clothes away. We believe that we should hand them in to you?" Frederick Tate said to them, as they made their way back into the police station before they gestured for Frederick Tate and Jennifer Lennon to take a seat.

"I don't suppose you caught a description of the people concerned?" Officer Daisy Campbell-Edwards wondered if they could provide some important information for this case.

"I'd say that they were roughly the height of your colleague with a slim build and brown coloured hair." Frederick shared some insight with the pair of them while Officer Dobson bagged the two costumes inside an evidence bag.

"I'm six – feet tall, and by the sounds of things we don't have much to go on since most of the people in this town have brown-coloured hair." Officer Dobson admitted that things would be tough to go on, and with that Officer Campbell-Edwards handed out two cups of tea for the UFO investigator and his assistant.

"I think that we should probably fill them in?" Officer Campbell-Edwards suggested to Officer Dobson who felt that since the investigation into this particular - part of the UFO incident had reached a conclusion, he didn't have an issue with.

"We've just come back from a farm along with your friends in manner of speaking, the Men in Black. The farmer at the farmhouse sighted a figure cloaked in black situated at his window. The farmer concerned aimed his shotgun at the figure who quickly pulled a disappearing act. We found footprints at the window after the Men in Black shone a torch over the area and to everyone's relief it was found to be of human origin." Officer Rhys Dobson said to them and with that Frederick Tate put two and two together.

"We could've captured the culprits had we known about this sooner?" Jennifer suddenly exclaimed and with that Frederick sat there ruefully drinking what remained of his tea before it got cold.

"What happens next?" Frederick suggested to the police officers who thought that all things considered everything had been done here.

"We've concluded this part of our investigation. We're now going to have to wait and see what happens next, but we're open to hearing about it as and when it occurs." Officer Daisy Campbell-Edwards informed them, and with that Frederick realised that he couldn't ask for much more than that.

Chapter Five

Confrontation

The following morning, Zodiac Isaac was pacing around the black-coloured car while waiting for one of his colleagues to show his face.

"I'm sure that there's nothing to be too concerned about, Zodiac. I'm sure he just overslept?" The man sat behind the wheel announced his suggestion in hopeful fashion, but Zodiac just shook his head before checking his watch.

"He knows what time we're heading out today. Go in there and get him out here." Zodiac ordered the man behind the wheel who quickly got out of the car before making his way back into the guest house.

"Good morning again, Mia. I was just wondering if my friend had put - in an appearance today?"

The man hoped that this had been a fruitful mission, but Mia shook her head before leading them towards the door where his colleague was meant to be staying.

"Do you want me to go in there first or do you want to be the one to head in there to see him? He might be in a case of undress?" Mia wondered what the man made of her remarks and with that the man headed into the room where he found it empty.

"He's not here Mia, you are free to enter the room." The man called out and with that Mia made her way into the room where she looked concerned and troubled.

"This is a bit odd. I thought that I saw him this morning going out for a stroll, but by the looks of things he never came back again." Mia explained to him, and with that the man realised that he had to report his colleague as being lost to Zodiac Isaac, which was something he wasn't looking forward to.

"Zodiac! I've got some important news to share with you." The man suddenly called out to him, and with that Zodiac turned around in – order to show he had his attention here.

"What's happening and why have you returned alone?" Zodiac hoped that his colleague had some decent answers to hand, because while there were only two of them, they were holding up the investigation.

"I asked Mia behind the front desk if she could show me to his room, but after entering the room it was discovered empty. She also told me that she saw him earlier today going out for a morning stroll around Broad Haven." The man brought him up to speed and with that Zodiac Isaac cut a frustrated figure while looking left and then right.

"That's an unauthorised absence, and - also the last thing we need right now. When we find him, I'm going to warn him that this sort of thing won't be tolerated in the future." Zodiac said to his driver before they decided to drive around the town while keeping a close lookout for their missing colleague.

Meanwhile Frederick Tate and Jennifer Lennon had entered their hotel dining room where they discovered Daniel Price and Kelly Evans waving them to join them at their table.

"Good morning to you both. Have you made any progress in this case?" Frederick was eager to find out if they'd found out anything they'd yet to discover themselves, but by the looks of things they hadn't made the kind of progress they might've hoped for.

"We believe that we'll find something today, because the children will be back at school and after all they were the people who sighted the UFO last week?" Daniel suggested to Frederick who picked up a slice of buttered toast while contemplating the day ahead.

"Are you going to tell them about what happened last night with the two young people who had appeared at the farmer's window?" Jennifer sought to find out what Frederick Tate made of the idea since they obviously had a keen and eager audience.

"What happened last night? Did we miss anything?" Kelly was suitably intrigued and with that Frederick nodded his head back in their direction.

"We came across two young people who discarded some black coloured clothing, which we picked up. We made our way over towards the police station just in case it was important, but we found to our interest that those that had discarded the clothing had appeared in - all likelihood at the window of the farmer while trying to scare him." Frederick explained to Daniel and Kelly who thought that this sounded somewhat dangerous considering the circumstances.

"Don't farmer's arm themselves with guns though?" Kelly suggested to Frederick who thought that she seemed to be on the ball.

"That's right, and whoever it was had a shotgun aimed at them before they disappeared from the window. Talk about taking a risk, but I can't see the young man taking such a risk again especially due to the heightened talk around the town of UFO's and perhaps alien beings being present." Frederick pointed out to them, and with that

Daniel shook his head as he finished off his cup of coffee.

"The plan we have today is to go to the school?" Jennifer Lennon suggested to Frederick who thought that they'd have to tread carefully since they would be dealing with the people in charge of the school, and there's no guarantee they would let them talk to the witnesses once they got there.

Zodiac Isaac and his colleague driving the car had driven around most of Broad Haven - but had yet to discover what had become of their friend and colleague.

"Do you think that we should report him as being missing to the police, because this is very odd behaviour. He understands the mission." The man driving the car attempted to be helpful, and Zodiac took a deep sounding breath as he contemplated his response.

"That's an embarrassing thing to think, but right now what other choice do we have here?" Zodiac realised that the man that was driving the car was bang on with this idea, and with that they pulled up outside Broad Haven police station. They left the car behind some moments later before heading inside where they hoped to report their missing colleague. The station itself was quiet at this time of the day with just a handful of police officers inside the place.

"Good morning. What brings you to Broad Haven police station this morning." A rather chirpy sounding female officer asked the towering Man in Black, and after a deep breath he responded.

"We're currently on the lookout for one of our own. For some reason he absconded from the guest house we were staying in, and after having a tour of the town in our car we've found our search was somewhat fruitless." Zodiac Isaac leaned in and advised her and with that she wrote some information down on the notepad she had in front of her.

"What kind of timeframe are we talking about your friend has been missing for, because it's in my experience people do tend to turn up around Broad Haven." The police officer named Lily

Hollins did her best to show that the situation might not be as dire as it seemed.

"I'd like to think that way too, but we're here on a mission and no part of that mission said that you're meant to disappear from your superior officer." Zodiac informed her before looking, as she was still waiting for him to confirm the last time he saw his colleague.

"About the time estimate?" Officer Lily Hollins did her gently – gently approach and with that Zodiac looked over towards his junior colleague and gestured for him to take a seat while discussions were ongoing.

"I'd say that the last time we saw him was when we arrived in the guest house last night. The lady who runs the place let us know that she thought that she saw him go out for a walk or stroll as she put it, this morning. So, we're worried that he's been gone for numerous hours and it's just not like him to be missing in action." Zodiac pointed out to her, and with that her colleague Dafydd Morone decided to join the discussion while showing Lily Hollins some much – needed support.

"What did your friend look like? Also, what was he wearing at the time since this could be very helpful in terms of tracking him down." Officer Hollins pointed out to Zodiac who took another deep sounding frustrated breath, as he felt that they'd make better progress without the police at this point.

"He's wearing the same attire as myself. Black coloured suit and matching black coloured hat. We've got no other clothes to wear while we're here in Broad Haven unless of course he's gone shopping without our knowledge." Zodiac informed them, and with that Lily had one final question she wanted answered from him.

"How was your relationship with your friend before you were separated with him? Were you getting on or did you have some heated words or something?" Lily suggested to Zodiac who felt that all things they were getting on about as well as they usually did.

"We were getting on just about fine. I'm the boss and he obeyed my command, isn't that - right?" Zodiac hollered over towards his remaining colleague who placed a hand in the air to show that he wasn't wrong on that score.

"What we'll do is distribute leaflets around Broad Haven, because your friend might've become lost, or perhaps disorientated during his morning stroll. Don't worry we've got a good record of tracking people down." Officer Dafydd Morone confirmed for Zodiac who promptly nodded his head before leaving the station with his remaining colleague for company.

"What do you make of their hopes?" The man asked Zodiac moments before they got back into their black – coloured car.

"They didn't exactly fill me with hope, let's just put it that way." Zodiac admitted that he couldn't see how placing leaflets around the town would aid their cause to track down their colleague.

Frederick Tate, Jennifer Lennon, Kelly Evans and Daniel Price made their way towards the local school before they headed inside whereupon they found their presence not exactly welcome.

"What's going on here, you can't just turn up without an appointment. We're trying to run a school here." Mrs Helen Pitman pointed out to the collection of investigators who realised they might have a job on their hands just to talk to the witnesses.

"We just need to speak with the witnesses for a few minutes and then we'll leave in peace." Frederick Tate hoped his words would sooth her words, but moments later in walked the teacher Max Davies who was stunned to see them there at this hour of the day.

"You do know that those very same witnesses happen to be young children?" Max Davies felt all things considered they needed to keep this in mind, but Daniel Price was still hopeful an audience would be granted since he'd come up with a similar idea the other day.

"We're only asking for ten minutes then we'll leave you all alone." Daniel hoped his comments would mean something here, and with that Max Davies repented and decided that the best way for them to leave the place was to give them what they asked for.

"Fine. I'll arrange it shortly, in the meanwhile stay here with Helen and I'll call for you when the assembly is ready." Max Davies remarked and with that he made his way out of the office. Outside Zodiac Isaac and his colleague had also pulled up in their car before joining them all in the office.

"What's going on around here?" Zodiac hoped that someone had some words of wisdom here, and with that Frederick Tate realised it'd probably be for the best if it came from him.

"We're about to speak with the UFO witnesses from the other day. The children who saw the UFO to be precise. You are more than welcome to join us if you don't seek to take over proceedings?" Frederick Tate hoped he understood the point he was trying to make here and with that Zodiac grumbled back in his direction, as he digested the remarks and rules he needed to stick by.

"Fine just as long as you ask the important questions, I'll be happy to let you run with the ball in a manner of speaking." Zodiac confirmed for him, as they made their way into the main hall of the school where they found the class full of students already waiting for them along with Max Davies who gestured for them to start when they were ready to begin.

"Hello everyone. My name's Frederick Tate and I'm here today to ask you about unusual craft that you might've seen in the sky outside some days ago. Did you see anything unusual at the time, and I'd like a show of hands if you did?" Frederick Tate hoped that they wouldn't be shy about this, and some moments later numerous hands shot into the air.

"Yes. What did you see and I'm talking about the girl in the green jumper?" Frederick thought all in all she looked like a credible witness to his mind while Zodiac Isaac stood next to him stroking his own chin.

"There was a group of us, and we all saw something unusual. It was like a metallic spinning disc like object, which we saw for what seemed like minutes. Are you here to tell us what it was?" The girl asked him in hopeful fashion, and with that Frederick Tate felt all eyes suddenly looking in his direction.

"That sounds like a good question to me, but what do you make of it, Frederick Tate?" Zodiac Isaac found the accusation to be somewhat amusing causing the UFO investigator to understand that this was a question he really couldn't answer.

"Unfortunately, I'm not in a position currently to give any definitive answers, but we are currently running with the idea that it was something that could be explained." Frederick shared some insight with the girl who'd asked him the question although she wasn't the only one who felt letdown by his answer.

"So, you don't know what we saw either?" The girl realised and felt that this sounded like a bit of a wasted opportunity to her mind.

"That's what we're here to find out." Frederick said to her and with that Zodiac Isaac took the opportunity to speak up and disclose what he'd got on his mind.

"We believe, well not all of us. Most of us are of the opinion that what you saw has simply disappeared never to be seen again. We feel that what you saw was a military object, that hasn't as

- yet been confirmed by the local Royal Air Force barracks in Brawdy." Zodiac explained to them and with that the students seemed pleased by his remarks and the meeting was promptly ended with Max Davies telling the students to go back to their classes.

"I trust everything is fine now?" Max Davies turned his attention back to the group of people stood next to him, and with that they indicated that the incident seemed to be of natural causes to them.

Zodiac Isaac and his colleague made their way out to their black coloured car situated outside the building when Frederick Tate had something on his mind, that couldn't wait.

"Just out of interest Mr Zodiac? Where's your other colleague the man who seemed to be on the ball when he spoke?" Frederick suggested to Zodiac while upsetting the man who was still in his company by his use of such remarks.

"He disappeared from the guest house this morning without telling us where he was going, as of right now we don't have a location for his specific whereabouts." Zodiac thought that he might as well tell him since he wasn't the type to let things drop.

"In the last few days this place has had a UFO sighting, a possible alien sighting at a farmhouse and now one of the Men in Black that has been called here to check things out disappear without a trace? This mystery is just running and running, isn't it?" Frederick Tate wondered what the most experience member of the Men in Black made of the situation they found themselves in here.

"Don't worry if he doesn't turn up soon then we'll leave him behind and he'll have to make his own way back again. Nothing gets in the way of the mission, and as you know these types of incidents happen more often than people think." Zodiac Isaac pointed out to him, and with that they made their way towards their guest house to see if the missing man had turned up yet.

"That's really - unusual, isn't it? I mean for a Man in Black to disappear on a mission, that's not something I've heard about before?" Jennifer Lennon suggested to Frederick who understood where she was coming from here, and with that they walked away from the school along with Daniel Price and Kelly Evans for company.

"So, did you buy that back there Frederick?" Daniel sought to find out if he agreed with Zodiac Isaac's reading of the situation was military based.

"You mean about Brawdy Royal Air Force base being somewhat responsible for the UFO the children noticed in the sky?" Frederick suggested to him, and with that he nodded his head to show that was what he was referring to.

"That would be it." Daniel confirmed for him, and with that Frederick promptly stopped walking moments before they looked around the sky above their heads in – order to see if there was anything about the place, but it was eerily clear on this Welsh winter's day.

"In someways it makes sense, and in that circle - I'll give Zodiac Isaac his due since he certainly placed all the children at their ease with his remarks. Although, having said that I didn't get the opportunity to ask him if he thought that it was a military based incident himself. I've got a feeling that he was only sent here to clear up the cloudiness in people's minds." Frederick shared with them, and with that they once again started to walk along the lanes back to their hotel where they hoped to get a bite to eat.

Meanwhile the Men in Black were making their way along with the street at the specified driving limit.

"That man was trying to get under your skin back there?" The man driving the car wondered what Zodiac Isaac made of the remarks made by Frederick Tate.

"I think I'm used to him by now, and you might've seen that I didn't entertain him in the way he'd been hoping, did I?" Zodiac reminded him that he'd batted away his intrusive remarks on their missing colleague.

"What happens if our colleague isn't back at the guest house?" The man driving the car sought to find out what the next stage of the plan was in that case.

"We'll have to cross that bridge when it comes to it, but I meant what I said back there if he's not at the guest house or at the police station then we'll have to leave him behind, because our mission will continue with or without him." Zodiac informed him, as they pulled up outside their guest house with them quickly getting out of their vehicle and making their way inside where they found the landlady called Mia situated, and she greeted them with a warm smile, something they didn't reciprocate.

"Good afternoon to you. Did you happen to see our colleague come back into the guest house while we were away in town today?" Zodiac asked her in hopeful fashion, and with that she nodded her head before showing them into his guest room where the other Man in Black was lying down on his bed in some degree of discomfort.

"He arrived about thirty – minutes or so ago. I don't know where he'd been or what he'd been up to, but he looked like he was dead on his feet when he came back into the guest house. He asked about you though, but I didn't know where you were going or what you were doing. He retired to his room, and he's been here ever since." Mia pointed out to them before she excused herself while Zodiac paced impatiently about the room while his other colleague watched on.

"I wonder what happened to him or where he's been?" The other Man in Black suggested to Zodiac who thought all things considered the only way they would be getting any answers to these questions was to wake the man up from his slumber.

"Wake up now." Zodiac ordered the man on the bed before he kicked the bed in some degree of frustration, and with that the man on the bed opened his eyes to see what was going on.

"Hello? What's happening?" The Man in Black on the bed hoped that someone or something would fill him in here, and with that he looked up at the towering figure of Zodiac Isaac who seemed to be hovering over him.

"Where have you been and what have you been up to? We've been back to the school and told the witnesses, that what they witnessed was military based and there was nothing to be too concerned about. Now what we want to know is where you went early this morning and why you felt the need to not let us know where you were going?" Zodiac hoped that the Man in Black would promptly fill in the missing blanks here, and with that the man gulped as he realised, he was in trouble with his boss.

"I woke up early after finding it troubling to sleep. I thought that going for an early morning walk would help me clear the cobwebs, but I must've got lost around here without the car and I couldn't find my way back to the guest house again." The Man in Black confirmed for him before he sat up on the bed while Zodiac Isaac was mulling over his remarks.

"That doesn't explain where you've been for all this time, because according to the landlady you've only been in for around half an hour. So, where have you been and what were you doing during that time?" Zodiac was waiting for information to emerge while his other colleague was watching on from the doorway.

"I became lost and made my way to the police station, and while I was there - they noticed that I matched a description of the man they were looking for. Apparently - you reported me as being missing in action, Zodiac?" The man on the bed suggested to him, and with that he nodded his head to show that he wasn't wrong.

"How did you get back to the guest house since you couldn't find your way before, could you?" Zodiac was like a dog with a bone here and wasn't about to let things drop even for his beleaguered looking colleague.

"The police were kind enough to drive me here. I think that they were just happy to close the book on a missing person's case." The man on the bed pointed out to Zodiac Isaac who realised that perhaps they were on the same page after all. The Men in Black left the guest house for the final time some hours later safe in the knowledge that they'd poured cold water on another UFO mystery, but had they since the case was still considered open almost fifty years later...

The End

Printed in Great Britain
by Amazon